P9-CFO-654

I Can Read!

READING 2 WITH HELP

MILDRED
and
SAM
Go to School

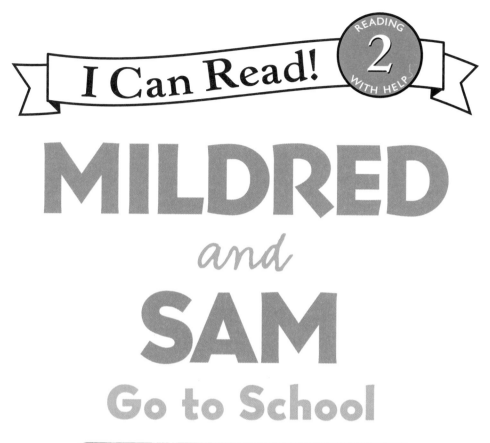

by Sharleen Collicott

LAURA GERINGER BOOKS

An Imprint of HarperCollinsPublishers

HarperCollins®, 📖®, and I Can Read Book® are trademarks of HarperCollins Publishers Inc.

Mildred and Sam Go to School
Copyright © 2008 by Sharleen Collicott
www.icanread.com

Library of Congress Cataloging-in-Publication Data
Collicott, Sharleen.
    Mildred and Sam go to school / by Sharleen Collicott.— 1st ed.
        p.   cm. — (An I can read book)
    Summary: After learning about caterpillars, frogs, and the planets for school, Mildred and Sam's eight little mice children have
wonderful dreams about each topic.
        ISBN-10: 0-06-058114-X (trade bdg.) — ISBN-10: 0-06-058115-8 (lib. bdg.)
        ISBN-13: 978-0-06-058114-5 (trade bdg.) — ISBN-13: 978-0-06-058115-2 (lib. bdg.)
        [1. Mice—Fiction. 2. Dreams—Fiction. 3. Schools—Fiction.] I. Title. II. Series.
PZ7.C67758Mn 2008   2005017885
[E]—dc22   CIP
                                                                                                                                                            AC

1   2   3   4   5   6   7   8   9   10   ❖   First Edition

CONTENTS

SHOW-AND-TELL

The little mice
were starting school.

"Good-bye," said Mildred.
"Be careful."
"See you later," said Sam.

"Oh dear. School is very far away,"
said Mildred.
"It is not that far," said Sam.

"Good morning,"
said Mrs. Sunnyseed.
"Welcome
to the first day of school."

The little mice played games.
They built a big jungle
out of paper and glue.

Mildred and Sam
peeked in the window.
They wanted to be sure
the little mice were having fun.

"Tomorrow,

we will have show-and-tell,"

Mrs. Sunnyseed said.

"Bring something special

to show the class."

After school,

the little mice

looked for something special

for show-and-tell.

They looked behind their burrow
and found some pebbles.
"Too boring," the little mice said.

They looked under the leaves
and found some ladybugs.
"Too small," the little mice said.

They looked behind a fern
and saw a giant caterpillar.
"Perfect!" the little mice said.

They made a leash out of vines
and took the caterpillar home.

Mildred and Sam

looked at the giant caterpillar.

"Be careful!" Mildred said.

"Keep that caterpillar

away from my garden."

"Remember," Sam said,

"that caterpillar

will turn into a moth someday."

That night,

the little mice dreamed

the giant caterpillar

ate Mildred's garden.

Then the caterpillar

turned into a moth.

The moth flapped his wings.

"Hello, little mice," he said.

"What are you doing out here?"

The little mice said,

"We are looking for something special

to take to show-and-tell."

"Not me!" said the moth,

and he flew away into the wind.

Before school,

Mildred and Sam and the little mice

took the caterpillar

back to the fern.

Then they filled a basket

with ladybugs

for show-and-tell.

Mildred and Sam

walked the little mice to school.

A few ladybugs flew away.

No one noticed.

Then a few more flew away.

When it was time
for show-and-tell,
there was only one ladybug
left in the basket.

"Here is our show-and-tell,"
the little mice said.
"We had a giant caterpillar,
but we let him go.
Then we had a whole basket
full of ladybugs.
But this is the only one
who wanted to come to school."

FIELD TRIP

The little mice
were going on a field trip.

"Oh dear," said Mildred.
"The pond is very far away."

"It is not that far," said Sam.
"Have a good time!"

"Good morning,"

Mrs. Sunnyseed said.

"We are going to the pond

to see the lily pads."

The little mice and their friends
bounced up and down
on the lily pads.
They bounced so high,
they landed in the water.

"What have we learned
about lily pads?"
Mrs. Sunnyseed asked her class.

The little mice looked around.

They looked under the lily pad
and saw a fish.
"It is so bright,"
the little mice said.

They looked above the lily pad
and saw a bird.
"It is so high,"
the little mice said.

They looked in the mud
and saw a tadpole.
It flicked its tail
at the little mice.
"It is so fast!"
the little mice said.

They swam in the pond
with the tadpole.

"Remember," Mrs. Sunnyseed said,
"that tadpole will turn into
a frog someday."

38

The little mice played
with the tadpole.
But it swam too fast.

So the little mice
took a nap on the lily pads
in the sun.

They dreamed the tadpole
turned into a giant frog.
The frog croaked loudly.

"Hello, little mice," he said.
"What are you doing out here?"

The little mice said,
"We are learning about lily pads."

"I am not a lily pad!"
the frog said, hopping away
with a big splash.

The splash woke the little mice
from their nap just in time.
The field trip was almost over!

"Swim to Mrs. Sunnyseed,"
the little mice said.
"Swim fast!"

Mildred and Sam came
to take the wet little mice home.

"How was the field trip?"
asked Sam.

"We learned about frogs,"
said the little mice.

"Were you careful?"
asked Mildred.

The little mice just smiled.

THE PLANETS

The little mice were ready
for a special lesson.

"Be careful," said Mildred.

"We will see you after school,"
said Sam.

"Good morning,"
Mrs. Sunnyseed said.
"Today, I will teach you
about the planets."

The little mice
looked at the sky charts
on the wall.
They made their own charts.

"Which planet
would you want to visit?"
Mrs. Sunnyseed asked the class.

The little mice
looked at the sky charts.

They looked close to the sun
and found Mercury.
"Too hot," the little mice said.

They looked next to Earth
and found Mars.
"Too red," the little mice said.

Then they saw Saturn,
circled by rings.
"Perfect," the little mice said.

The little mice
decided to visit Saturn.

"Okay," Mrs. Sunnyseed said,
and she gave them a star
on their work sheet.

After school, the little mice
told Mildred and Sam
that they wanted to go to Saturn.

"Be careful," said Mildred.
"Saturn is very far away."

"And you never know
who you might meet in space,"
said Sam.

"We are not scared,"
the little mice said.

That night,

the little mice dreamed

they were sailing in a sky boat.

They sailed between the stars.

"Hello, little mice,"

the stars said.

"What are you doing out here?"

The little mice said,

"We are going to visit Saturn."

"Be careful," the stars said.

"There are sky kittens on Saturn!"

When the little mice
landed on Saturn,
they saw the sky kittens
looking at them.

"Turn the sky boat around!"
the little mice said.
"Sail for home! Sail fast!"

Before school,

Sam gave the little mice

a present.

It was a rocket ship,

just the right size

for little mice.

"Now you can visit Saturn,"

said Sam.

"Even though it is very far away,"

said Mildred.

"No!" said the little mice.
"We want to stay right here at home
for now."

They jumped into their rocket ship
and sped off to school.

"Compared to Saturn," said Mildred,
"school is not so far away
after all."